William Heinemann

The First Step

A Dramatic Moment

William Heinemann

The First Step
A Dramatic Moment

ISBN/EAN: 9783337342098

Printed in Europe, USA, Canada, Australia, Japan

Cover: Foto ©Andreas Hilbeck / pixelio.de

More available books at **www.hansebooks.com**

THE FIRST STEP
A DRAMATIC MOMENT
BY
WILLIAM HEINEMANN

" Facilis descensus Averni"

LONDON
JOHN LANE AT THE SIGN OF THE
BODLEY HEAD IN VIGO STREET
MDCCCXCV

TO HER WHOSE
INTEREST AND ENTHUSIASM
INSPIRED
THIS EFFORT

NOTE

It has not been the object of the author to write anything that would satisfy the usual requirements of a stage play with regard to variety and action—but simply to snatch one dramatic moment out of a story of to-day, and to observe in its treatment economy as well as the dramatic unities.

THE PERSONS OF THE PLAY

FRANK DONOVAN

JACK DURWEN

ANNIE ⎫
⎬ Sisters
LIZZIE ⎭

This edition consists of 500 *copies*

THE SCENE OF THE PLAY

A large sitting-room in a lodging-house. Folding doors at back leading into bedroom. Next to them a smaller door leading to landing. Two windows on left. Upright piano between. On the right-hand side in the front, writing-table and chair, then fireplace with sofa facing it. Between fireplace and door a small sideboard. In centre of room, somewhat to the left, dining-table with chairs.

Time

First Act, about Mid-day

Second Act, during the Afternoon

Third Act, between three and four on the following morning

THE FIRST STEP

FIRST ACT

FIRST ACT

Breakfast things are still on the table, although the
meal has been finished for some considerable
time. The daily papers are strewed about on the
floor, and the room bears an untidy appear-
ance. FRANK *discovered deep in thought, sitting at*
the writing-table, nibbling his pen. During the
Act he lights one or two cigarettes. He is dressed
in a morning suit.

FRANK

I shall never get this scene right, and I should so
much like to do just what she asks. It may spoil
the play. But then. Let me see what she says in
her letter. "The fault seems to me in the weak-
"ness of the climax; you work up to a certain effect
"which you don't reach. The whole thing is, from
"the beginning, perfectly built up and the attention
"is so thoroughly held, that it is essential there
"should be no falling off. You prepared one all
"through the play for a tremendous situation by
"piling effect on effect; and, in fact, the situation is
"there, but if you will read over the words you have
"put into the mouth of the revengeful woman, you

" must see that, spoken as they are written, they can
" never produce on an audience the effect you desire.
" Let me draw a parallel with your last play, and
" remind you of the last act of ' Lucy Frail.' " Lucy
Frail! Ah, yes; that was written under very different
circumstances, under very different circumstances,
before I knew you, Madonna; when all seemed such
plain sailing, and there were only Annie and myself in
the wide world. [*Silence—takes up pen—puts it down
again—opens drawer—takes out photograph—loses
himself in contemplation.*] How can I put words, fit
for the she-devil in this play, into your mouth—into
such a mouth! Ye gods! Had I but never seen
this face! I hate it—and perhaps I know—but
shame on you, Frank Donovan, the Rising Light, the
fin de siècle Shakespeare! Shame! Shame on you!
Pull yourself together! What does this mean?
Yes, what the devil does it mean?

> [ANNIE *has entered and is removing the breakfast
> things—has watched him for a few moments,
> but has only caught the last word or two
> as she has moved to the head of his chair.
> She catches sight of the photograph over his
> shoulder and suppresses a movement of pain.
> She lays her hand on his shoulder, apparently
> unconcerned, caressingly.*

ANNIE

What is it, Frank, what is it? Are you not well,

dearest? Confide in your little mouse. You know that she will do anything for you, anything to help to make you happy. You know you have promised to share everything with her. How can you withhold rightly what is hers—half of your secrets. Tell me, Frank, tell me what is troubling you?

FRANK

Nothing, dear, nothing, nothing is the matter. What should be the matter? It is only that scene, that last scene. Mrs. Courtree complains of it; says it is weak and ineffective—says I miss the climax. The worst of it is, that I think she is right, and yet for the life of me I don't see how I am to change it so as to satisfy her.

ANNIE

How can she, Frank! How dare she find fault with your work! If she can't act that scene, there are many who can.

FRANK

You forget, dearest, that the play is written for her—to her order—and that I must do my best to please her.

ANNIE

You won't spoil your work for her sake! To suit

3

her whims! To avoid showing her weakness! If she is unable to act the part you have written, if she cannot realise and reproduce on the stage the creature of your imagination, you won't on that account treat your character like a tailor's misfit and alter and cut it about. If you change it, Frank, it will show the alterations. The seams will be awry, the buttons won't correspond with their holes, and the thing will hang in folds and ugly creases. Don't touch it, Frank—don't!

FRANK

Ah, but I must, dearest.

ANNIE

You must *not!* You *must* nothing! You are engaged to produce a work of art, not a thing of shreds and patches! You have created a work of art. They cannot withhold your pay.

FRANK

They are not at all likely to do that.

ANNIE

Then why should you care? Why should you listen to her complaints? You will not—you cannot write down to the level of her puny intellect. She

4

is bound to produce the play; if it shows up her own littleness, that won't affect you.

FRANK

She might suppress the play, pay me, and let it be understood that the thing had turned out such a disappointment that no sane person would risk a sovereign to produce it.

ANNIE

But they would never believe that—never! How could they, after the praise they have showered upon you? After the fuss they have made of you as the rising dramatist of our time? Just fancy what fools they would appear!

FRANK

Ah, my dear, I fear that consideration would never affect a critic. He is too well accustomed to the part. Criticism, particularly dramatic criticism, is the art of eating your own words. The idol of to-day is the laughing-stock of to-morrow. They praise you once, because of the momentary sensation that is caused by a new discovery. But their *amour-propre* does not allow them to praise you twice. When your second play is produced the novelty that attaches to discovering you is worn off. They are on the look-out for, if they have not already discovered a new idol,

5

and you are pityingly assured that you are a one-play-man, that you will never write another equal to your first.

ANNIE

Frank, I could never live to see you degraded, or laughed at by those who now patronise you—yes, and praise and extol you to heaven.

FRANK

It is for this very reason that I must first of all give satisfaction to my employers. Some day, perhaps, who knows, I may have a position making me independent of any one—when I can live for my art and my art alone. At present I am forced to consider those who pay me, those who employ, those who judge me. And, if necessary, I must succeed, notwithstanding my critics. One successful play is so easily explained away. If my second performance pleases less than my first, they will unhesitatingly put me back, and I shall have to fight the whole battle over again. I should have but scanty consideration from the whole gang who toady to me to-day. Too much depends upon it, Annie—for both of us. We must succeed—you and I ; and to do so I must please, first of all.

ANNIE

It is sometimes this very responsibility that you

feel towards me that frightens me, Frank. Sometimes you appear oppressed by its weight, and you feel the necessity of immediate success on my account more than on your own.

FRANK

Nonsense, Annie, nonsense !

ANNIE

You are so good, Frank. You fancy that you owe to me more than to yourself, to your genius, to your ambition, that you should succeed with this play—succeed in the worldly sense. Oh, Frank, that feeling is terrible. If you could only be free to do as your genius commands. I have given up so much for your sake.

FRANK

I know, I know ! Why remind me ?

ANNIE

If aught remains to me of myself you know that I would gladly, willingly, freely, give that up as well—sacrifice my whole self—if I could buy your independence. You have my happiness, my love, my life. Can I help you further ? Indeed, can I help you—help you to fulfil your mission—to realise this ideal of *our* life—and never, never be a hindrance in your path ? Be yourself, Frank. Give your own work and yours alone. I would never have done what I have done, and I could never do what I would willingly do in the future, should occasion demand it, if I thought that you would degrade yourself to write a play simply to please the rabble—to fill the coffers of a manager, and leave you on no higher platform than the rest of them, who write to amuse and tickle, for effect, and with no higher soul and no higher ambition than the making of money, and money only.

FRANK

You are as eloquent about things you don't understand as you are unreasonable. There is no idea of such a thing; it has never entered my mind. In the first instance, I wrote what came into my head. Poor in experience of the practical requirements of the stage, I wrote certain lines. When they were spoken —spoken by an eminent actress—one whose genius the world acknowledges, whom you yourself at one time thought able more than any other to represent my character—they sounded out of proportion, and did not realise the very thing which I had hoped to realise. I am now asked to take the advice of old and experienced heads, and I am trying to remodel this poor little play of mine in the light of their greater wisdom. No, indeed, one scene and one scene only—merely to remodel it to suit the requirements

8

of the footlights, which are to me, of course, at present somewhat of a *terra incognita*.

ANNIE

[*Who is lost in thought—absently.*] Frank! Do you remember the evening when you wrote that scene? I see it as clear as if it had been yesterday. It was all planned out before, and you had waited from day to day for a moment when you could sit down with the confidence that sometimes fills you in your work, to write it. It was a Sunday, and we had been up the river with Lizzie and Jack. It was the first time those two had met; and when we got back to the station he wanted to see her home. But we took her home ourselves; and when we got to the dear old house I hid in the back of the four-wheeler, not to let mother see me—mother who had not seen me since the day when I came away with you. But mother did see me—bless her! and she came out and forced me in with Lizzie. You would not stay, and excused yourself.

FRANK

I came home and worked.

ANNIE

Yes, yes! You went home; but I went in again among them all. They seemed to have become

9   B

strange, hardly knowing how to approach me, for I was in disgrace with father, and had been held up to the little ones as a shocking example. Father could not forgive me. He was away at the time, else mother would not have dared to bring me in. Poor dear mother—if she had known all, would she have been so good, so kind to me?—could she have forgiven that I was not as she? She could never have seen it all from my point of view—she could not have understood. It seemed wrong of me to go in there among them ; but I could not resist the temptation to see them again and to feel for a moment that I was one of them. When after a while I realised the deceit of it, when my eyes fell on this ring, which was there a solemn lie to them all, I felt faint, and had to go out into the air—back to you—to you, Frank.

FRANK

You did not stay long there.

ANNIE

I found you here writing, and I sat motionless and watched you for hours. All was as quiet as could be, and you were writing away furiously—lost entirely in your work. At times I could not stifle my sobs, and I feared you would notice me ; but at length I grew calmer, and I listened to the noise of your pen, and that was the best music in the world. It soothed me like a lullaby, and changed all bitterness to joy. I was so happy. Tears came to me foolishly, all of pleasure and love for you. At last, when you had done, you turned round to me and found me there. You were surprised to see me, for you had thought yourself alone. Unconsciously, you said, my presence had given you fire and strength. You had written that scene and you were proud of it, and declared it was the best piece of work you had ever done. I had inspired it, you said, and when you read it to me, I cried again—bitterly. You laughed at me, I remember, and kissed me as you had never kissed me before. So—so—Frank [*kissing him passionately*]—that is how you kissed me! We were very near to one another that evening.

FRANK

[*Impatiently.*] But we are always the same, you goose. Always the same.

ANNIE

You seemed so great—so unapproachably great, and I was so small, so insignificant. It was as it used to be in those first days when we met at the Academy of Music. You were the pride, the show pupil of the place, and I was trying so hard to develop my poor little voice with scale practices. You used to come in and listen to me, and although you were kind

11

and encouraged me, I knew well enough how poorly you thought of it all. You used to wait for me and accompany me home. Music did not satisfy you, although you excelled in it. You envied those who were free to follow the bent of their genius, and you wanted so much to be a great writer, one whose name would be on everybody's tongue. How well I remember those walks when you first told me your plans, of the position you hoped to conquer, and you said that I—I only—could help you to do so. It was like a new world to me, and I was proud that you had chosen me to confide in—me of all the others. Oh, Frank, those were very happy days!

FRANK

And these? Are we not always the same? Ever since you left your parents and came to me, because we were indispensable to one another. Have we not always been the same? And just as you have given up and sacrificed so much for our common cause, have I not also done everything in my power to achieve that success, that assurance, which—which——

ANNIE

[*Interrupting*]—which would enable you to quite fulfil your promise—to make me an honest woman. I know, Frank; I know; you are good, and I am silly; but it sometimes overcomes me—this feeling—

lately, perhaps, more than ever. Forgive me, Frank.
At times I am almost jealous of the attention you
seem to be compelled to pay to Mrs. Courtree.
When she sends for you, you go to see her, by night
or day, and what she asks, you are bound to do.
Sometimes that seems unreasonable to me. It—it
pains me; but then I reflect, and I know that
you love me, that you must love me, with all
your heart—with all your heart, Frank. Me, and
me only.

FRANK

Of course, you silly little goose, of course I do.
Mrs. Courtree! Ha! ha! "What's Hecuba to me,
or I to Hecuba!"

ANNIE

[*Rises as if to go. She picks up a tray, puts
it down again.*] Frank, you will remember to-day.
Lizzie is coming. Is Jack coming also?

FRANK

I hope so. I wrote and asked him. There is no
reply; but you know how careless he is about answer-
ing letters. I told him Lizzie would be here, and I
fancy that will bring him. But he would come to-day
anyhow—to-day of all days. He knows how much
we want him to-day.

13

ANNIE

Frank, dear, do you know I am a little frightened
of Jack sometimes—am I unreasonable? I fancy
sometimes that he is not so good a friend now as he
used to be, that there is something interested in his
friendship. His pretended infatuation for Lizzie—is
it an honest love? How can he want to marry her?
Rich as he is, and she poor. He—so well versed in
the ways of the world—a man about town, with his
clubs and his friends, and always in a rush of pleasure
and excitement. She, a simple, pretty, inexperienced
little girl, who has seen nothing, been nowhere, with
only her own family circle and a few school friends.
You know how strict we were kept at home.

FRANK

I know—too much Nonconformist conscience about
the place.

ANNIE

Father would allow us to go nowhere, not even to an
innocent dance or to a theatre. Duty, obedience, and
piety, how often have I heard those words from his
lips, until I got tired and weary, and life in its grey
dullness seemed so intolerable—until you came into
it. Lizzie has been kept even stricter than I was
kept, since I, in father's words, "went wrong." You
spoke to me first of what is noble and great, of the

14

freedom of thought, of the beauty of an independent mind, and of art, holy, glorious art! Yes, you were my saviour, my bringer of light, my own dear Frank. But Jack!

FRANK

And why should not Jack be the same to Lizzie? Why should he not make her happy? He is a good friend, he has always been a good friend, and I owe him so much—gratitude. Jack's very fond of Lizzie, and he is wealthy, which is, after all, half the battle of life!

ANNIE

He is not like you, Frank; he is very different—a man of pleasure He cannot desire Lizzie for his wife.

FRANK

Well, and if he does not, what harm is there in an innocent flirtation? He is a good friend—is Jack!

ANNIE

Frank, how can you say such things—how!—men like Jack don't waste their time on little suburban *belles* without an object. You must help me to prevent their meeting too often. Frank, you will, won't you, dearest?

15

FRANK

And what excuse can I make to Jack? He has always been a good friend. I can't suddenly insult him, and besides, why should I? Perhaps he won't come to-day, and you will have changed your mind about him by to-morrow, little goose! She must not worry her stupid little brain about all sorts of nightmares. She must only think of nice, pretty things, and just dote on her own boy. Run along and get things ready. I know we shall have to wait ever so long for our dinner.

ANNIE

Very well, Frank. I love you and adore you! But you will keep an eye on them, won't you, dearest? There now—[*gets his hat*]—you go out and get a blow while I prepare for dinner.

[*She kisses him. Exit* ANNIE *with tray, while he lights cigarette. He goes to sideboard, takes glass of brandy.*

FRANK

[*Alone.*] Nuisance all this business. [*Putting up his papers at writing-table, picks up photo of Mrs. Courtree, loses himself in contemplation.*] If Annie does not get married soon . . . . you . . . . but no —must not think of you [*putting away picture*]—not think of you! [*Going towards door, where he meets*

16

LIZZIE.] Hullo! little 'un, little sister-in-law, how are we?

LIZZIE

I am very well, Frank. Hope you're the same. [*Laughs.*] Where is Annie?

FRANK

Oh, Annie is cooking and slaving away as usual. I will send her up to you. I am just going out; shall be back directly. Ta, ta. [*Exit.*
[LIZZIE *puts down small bag which she has carried; takes off her hat and arranges her hair in front of the mirror; takes a small parcel out of her bag.*

LIZZIE

I have a good mind to go down and help her. What a lovely time she must have here. Frank is so good to her, and none of the nagging of father and mother. I am getting tired of it. Barely enough pocket-money to dress yourself respectably. These gloves I have worn' for over two months—they are positively indecent, darned at every seam. I wish I could find some rich old man asleep whom it would take a brass band to awake. I'd kiss him for ten minutes— sixty to the minute—and make him give me enough gloves to enable me to show my hands outside of my muff all the rest of my life. [*Coquettishly looking at a very dainty little hand.*] I hate muffs—all sorts of muffs. Jack is not a muff. [*Laughs merrily.*]

[*Opens the piano and plays a few chords of a popular song.*

Enter ANNIE.

ANNIE

[*Kissing* LIZZIE.] Frank told me you were here. Why didn't you come down to me? You might have learnt how to make a custard. It's all done now. However, you can help me lay the cloth. How are they at home, dear? How is mother, and Dolly, and Tots?

LIZZIE

They are all right. Mother sends you this.

ANNIE

Oh, thanks, dear.

LIZZIE

Don't open it now; after dinner.

ANNIE

Very well, then; and how is——

LIZZIE

[*Interrupting.*] Father ? He actually asked after you the other day.

ANNIE

Did he though ?

LIZZIE

He has been reading in the *Review of Reviews* the Man of the Month—about Frank, and he seems quite interested in him. He didn't even object to my coming here—for the first time, and I may stay. There's my bag. Is Jack coming ?

Enter JACK.

JACK

Good morning.

LIZZIE

Well, I do declare ! Speak of the——

JACK

I have just looked in to answer Frank's note ; I only got it to-day. I shall be very happy to come in later. Have not seen Frank for ages.

ANNIE

Frank will be delighted, I feel sure.

19

JACK

It is almost time, I suppose; but I have just got to run up the street. I shall not be many minutes. Ah! There's Miss Lizzie, too; I hope quite well.

LIZZIE

Oh, yes; very well. I did hope we were going to have a quiet time here to-day. [JACK *laughs.*

JACK

There we are again, Sauce-box. [*Turning to* ANNIE.] That girl teases me and abuses me whenever she sees me. What have I done to her?

ANNIE

It strikes me, Mr. Durwen, that you two get on remarkably well, and that you don't suffer much from her sauce. You will excuse us, please, I must go to make myself look presentable, and Lizzie has got to lay the cloth for dinner.

JACK

Capital! Then I will show her how to do it. It is not very pressing, any way, my business; and I am quite certain that if Miss Lizzie is left alone she will give me nothing but knives [*Exit* ANNIE *shrugging her shoulders*], and I shall cut myself

20

with them, and she will laugh, having a whole handful of spoons to herself. I wonder, when I am badly hurt, whether she will give me just one spoon—will she?

LIZZIE

She will give you neither one thing nor the other. You shall stand in the corner and watch us eating, if you continue in your present behaviour. You are an impertinent, useless person, and may just as well go about your business. Let me lay the cloth.

JACK

Why certainly—only you might give me a trial. I am an excellent master—expert in these things, and you would get the advantage of being taught the art of making a table look attractive. Take this end of the table-cloth, spread it over here, and smooth out the creases. Now the flowers; no, stay, how many shall we be?

LIZZIE

Why, four of course, you silly.

JACK

Here Annie, and Frank opposite, you here and I here. No, that would not do; there would be the girls together and the men together—girl facing girl, and man facing man. It will give me a better appetite, because if I have your face to look at all the while, little cat, I shall forget all about the eating.

[*He has come close to her and put his arm round her ; she shakes him off.*

LIZZIE

Yes, it will be better for me, too, because if your face is opposite to mine I shall look persistently into my plate.

JACK

Then, I bet, you'll manage to get hold of one of these tin ones, and that you'll polish its surface so that it reflects your divine little mask.

LIZZIE

I wish you would go away and let me lay the cloth ; you are a positive nuisance.

JACK

Very well, then, I will; but before I go—I say, Lizzie, I have got a box for the Gaiety to-night: do you think we could manage to go ? Would they let us ? You know you want to go to the theatre —you have been wanting so long.

LIZZIE

Oh, I should like to go to the theatre; but, how

can I ? They are sure to find out at home. I don't know what father would do if he thought I had been to the play. He thinks the theatre so wicked, and yet Frank is something theatrical himself, is he not ? Why he wrote a play, and even that was "*strictly prohibited.*" I wish I dared to go.

JACK

They won't know. We can get you home early, just as if you had spent the evening here quietly.

LIZZIE

Oh, that does not matter because I am going to stay here over night. But Annie will never let me. She would not dare to. Father would never let me come here again. This is the first time I have come here to stay over night. I had to promise all sorts of things before I could get permission. I wanted so much to stay with my married sister. It does seem unreasonable to have a married sister and not to be allowed to stay with her. What else are married sisters for ?

JACK

[*Laughing.*] Yes, indeed. Good old married sisters !

LIZZIE

It was bad enough before Annie ran away and

23

got married without father's consent, but since then he is awful. We are hardly allowed out of sight, and in the evenings we have to read—*aloud*, mind you. If at least we could read to ourselves, one could have a nice exciting shocker inside the covers of the "Pilgrim's Progress." But we've got to read aloud to him, whether we like it or not. He is getting worse and worse. He hardly ever mentions Annie's name, just because they got married without asking him to the wedding. I *should* like to go, though. I shall never have another chance. Oh, Jack, it would be lovely. How aggravating!

JACK

We must make a plan of campaign together. Let's see! I will tell you what. We'll say nothing till after dinner, and then I'll broach the subject. I'll suggest our going all together.

LIZZIE

Yes, that will be the best. If I am with Annie, it can't be so awful. Oh, Jack, you are nice.

JACK

Am I, though, little miss ?   [*He goes up to her.*

LIZZIE

Go away, and let me lay the table.

JACK

I want a kiss before I go.

LIZZIE

Certainly not.

JACK

Well, I shall not go, then.

LIZZIE

You will go.

JACK

Well, I shall not take you to the play, then.

LIZZIE

Oh, Jack, you are aggravating!

JACK

A kiss or no play—which shall it be?

LIZZIE

Very well, then—but one only—and you will go immediately—promise.

JACK

Why, certainly. [*She holds her cheek and he kisses it.*] You don't call that a kiss.

LIZZIE

That is all you'll get, any way.

JACK

I am not going to take that—that's a counterfeit. I want the real article while I am about it—a bargain is a bargain.

LIZZIE

Are you a man of honour, Mister Jack, or are you not? You promised to go if I gave you a kiss, and you have had one.

JACK

I took one, you gave me nothing at all. You don't call that giving a kiss, do you? [*He comes near her and kisses her on the mouth.*] See, now I am satisfied. Adieu, my dear!

LIZZIE

You beast!

Enter ANNIE *from bedroom, having changed her gown and smartened herself.*

26

ANNIE

What ! you have not laid the table yet ?

LIZZIE

He has been doing nothing but making a fool of
himself and hindering me from getting on. I wish
you would tell him to go away. I have asked him to
do so all the time. If I had known he was coming I
should have stayed away.
> [JACK *makes a sign to* ANNIE *and goes out, saying,*
> *" Back directly."*

LIZZIE

What do you think of Jack, Annie ?

ANNIE

How do you mean, Lizzie ? He is a great friend of
Frank's. I like all his friends.

LIZZIE

I am so glad you like him, he is such fun.

ANNIE

Be careful, little sister. He is a man of the world
and perhaps he knows too much for you. I have
sometimes wanted him not to come here so often,
particularly when you were here; but Frank is so

infatuated with him that I dare not resist his coming.

LIZZIE

Oh! but has Frank paid him that money he owed him?

ANNIE

Money, Lizzie! What do you mean? Frank doesn't owe him any money.

LIZZIE

Oh yes he does, Jack told me so himself, and he said he would lend him as much more as ever he wanted. Jack is a good friend to Frank, I am sure of that.

ANNIE

[*In a brown study.*] But I wish Frank owed him no money. Horrible! horrible!

FRANK *enters, bringing flowers.*

FRANK

Here you are, little woman. [*Aside to her.*] This is our wedding-day, is it not? And here are some violets for Lizzie. Go in there, and put them on. Jack will like to see you with them on. [*Exit* LIZZIE.]

[*To* ANNIE.] Annie, my love, I have thought about it all again and again. It will not do for us to remain any longer as we are now. I want you to consent at once to our marriage—all will be better then, and there will not be all this double life. It must be now—at once—the sooner the better.

ANNIE

No, Frank, I dare not yet. You know we promised one another that nothing would tempt us to this step until your success was assured. You know that our marriage before you are independent of every one—with me, whom the world would look upon as unworthy of you—would hurt your prospects, perhaps ruin them. Besides, how could we afford to live in a way suitable to your position? We should have to go among your friends—your rich, your great friends. We are not ready for that—not until the play is out.

FRANK

Young people need not entertain their friends, and it will be better that they should all know.

ANNIE

We must keep to what we proposed—keep to what we have planned—keep to what we have lived for. We swore it so solemnly that nothing should tempt us to this step until the new play had been produced. If my faith ever had a doubt how could I feel myself purified again—able to look good women in the face unashamed? For me to marry you now would be to disbelieve you. You shall never have reason to say that I ever for one moment doubted you. You may distrust yourself, but I have faith in you. Your word is as good as your work, and that is the best in the land. It is only a few weeks more, and then all will be well. I can wait; I must wait. Surely you can. You risk—you can lose so little.

FRANK

But it is this uncertainty which is killing me; it is preventing me from working—this double life that I am leading. The evenings out in the world of pleasure and fashion — the nights and the days of quiet at home—the hiding the one from the other— the strain is too much. You must, you must be my wife. The world—they all, Mrs. Courtree and the rest of them—they shall know you, and I shall be proud to tell them how good, how loyal you were. You must, Annie—or I will not be responsible for the consequences.

ANNIE

Frank, there is something in the way you say that which frightens me—not on my account but on yours.

You can't afford now to marry me, and you would wish it undone the day after. We must keep our compact—at any cost—that promise we made one another.

FRANK

That promise! That promise! Confound our weakness which required a promise.

ANNIE

But, Frank, that promise was to be a help to us, to be true to our purpose, to enable us to carry out all our plans—a help, Frank, a help.

FRANK

I know! I know! How ludicrous! What seemed then a help is now an intolerable hindrance!

CURTAIN.

SECOND ACT

Dinner is over. JACK *and* LIZZIE *are still at the table talking ;* FRANK *is discovered stretched out on a sofa. He is flushed with wine, and excited, particularly towards the end of the Act.*

LIZZIE

Play us something, Frank. Something jolly, with a good rollicking tune. [*She gets up, and opens the piano.*] Come here ! don't be lazy.

[*He gets up, and comes to the piano.*

FRANK

What shall I play ?

LIZZIE

Anything you like, Frank.

JACK

Let us have some Chopin. You play Chopin so well. Anything of his—except the " Funeral March." [FRANK *plays,* JACK *thrumming the time on the table.*]

35

Capital! I'd give anything to play like you. Let's have a dance, Frank.

LIZZIE

Yes, yes! A waltz. The " Blue Danube," Frank. [*To* JACK.] Come ·on! Help us to push the table away. [*They push the dining-table towards the back, and move the chairs.* JACK *takes hold of* LIZZIE *and waltzes with her. Whilst he is waltzing, he kisses her; she immediately stops.*] There, I have had enough of you. If you weren't such a useless person, you would play the piano now for me and Frank to dance; but some people are made only to annoy.

FRANK

Ha, ha! She knows you, old boy. Never mind, we will dance without music.
                [*He whistles, and whirls her round twice.*

LIZZIE

[*Exhausted.*] I don't care to dance without music.

FRANK

I can't play the music and dance at the same time; so, if you can't dance with Jack, you must either dance without music, or do without dancing. Jack can't play a common scale.

36

LIZZIE

I am quite aware of that; neither can he dance.
Here is Annie. , I shall dance with her.

[ANNIE, *carrying a tray of coffee, stops at the
door and realises the scene.*

ANNIE

Well, I declare! You are having a good time;
and here have I been sacrificing myself to make you
coffee.   [*She puts down the coffee on the table.*

JACK

Come, Mrs. Donovan! Let's have a dance.   I
fancy you must dance ever so much better than Lizzie.
Sit down, Frank, and give us another tune.

[LIZZIE *goes up to table and pours out coffee while
they are dancing.*

ANNIE

[*Exhausted, stopping.*] That's enough; I am quite
out of breath. I have not danced for I don't know
how long.

LIZZIE

Oh, Annie, I want you to dance with me; Jack
can't dance a bit.

ANNIE

I thought he danced very well indeed.

LIZZIE

Oh, he slurs over all his steps; I don't call that dancing. I want to dance with you.

ANNIE

Let me have my coffee first; I am perfectly exhausted.
> [FRANK *sings—they all listen. Suddenly he breaks off.*

FRANK

What do you think of that?

JACK

Capital, capital!

ANNIE

Oh, do go on and finish it.
> [*She is rapt in listening.* JACK *goes up to* LIZZIE *and talks, while* FRANK *resumes song.*

FRANK

[*Finishing.*] Another time I will trouble you to be quiet while I sing. Schumann with his " Schlummerlied" has precious little chance against two aggravating gabblers like you. It's hot, fearfully hot in here, isn't it? [*Opening window.*] I wonder

whether I shall have to go to the theatre to-night.
There ought to be a wire soon, if I am wanted.

ANNIE

You are not going out to-night, Frank?

FRANK

I may have to go. One never knows what the
caprices of one's leading lady may be.

ANNIE

But you won't go to-night. Surely that woman
should have some consideration for your private
comfort!

FRANK

That woman, Mistress Jealous! How absurd you
are. *That* woman. Just look at her now! I may
have to go down to the theatre to settle some important business with Mrs. Courtree—about the gown
she is to wear in the last act, or some other tomfoolery.
And the mere mention of that woman's name upsets
our equilibrium. Observe my lady's face.

ANNIE

Oh, Frank! how can you! I did hope you would
stay at home to-night—to-night of all nights.

FRANK

So I shall in all probability; but *if* I am called away, I can't let domestic arrangements interfere with my business.

> [FRANK *goes on* playing a waltz. LIZZIE *wants to dance with* ANNIE.

ANNIE

No, no! I don't want to dance any more.

LIZZIE

But I wanted to dance with you.

ANNIE

No, dear; go and dance with Jack.

LIZZIE

No, I shan't. [JACK *comes up and catches hold of her.*

JACK

You shall!

> [*Forces her to dance. They whirl round; he kisses her again.* ANNIE *observes it.*

ANNIE

How dare you! What have you done?

40

FRANK

What's the matter ?

ANNIE

He has kissed Lizzie ?

JACK

Well, and what of that ?   She teases me to such an extent that I must find some means of avenging myself.

ANNIE

You have no right to kiss her.   [*To* LIZZIE.] How could you let him ?

LIZZIE

I didn't !   Never mind, if he does it again I shall scream.

ANNIE

I must trouble you, Mr. Durwen, to treat my sister as you would wish your own sister to be treated.
                                    [*She goes out of the room.*

LIZZIE

Annie is too absurd !   Not that I don't think you perfectly insulting and beastly !   [*Follows* ANNIE.

FRANK

[*Laughing.*] You have put your foot in it this time, old man. Why did you let Annie see it? If you want to kiss the girl, it won't hurt her: only Annie of late has been most intractable in her moods. I don't know what is the matter with her. She has completely changed—always referring to what those confounded people of hers would do and think. I can't make out what has come over her. She used to be entirely indifferent to the opinion of others, as long as I approved.

JACK

I say, Frank, I wanted you to come round to the Gaiety this evening; I have got a box. I thought the girls would like it. Don't you think they would come?

FRANK

How good of you! I'm not sure whether I shall be able to go. I'm never certain about Mrs. Courtree, you know. She may suddenly take it into her head that she wants to see me—consult about something or other—connected with the play [JACK *looks doubtful*]. I never know. She sends wires for me at all hours, and then I've got to leave everything and go off as fast as I can. However, if I should be called away, you can take the girls if you like—that is to say, if Annie will go. I don't suppose she will. You will be *tête-à-tête* with Lizzie—you won't mind that, will you, for once ?—although I don't for a moment pretend that a *tête-à-tête* is as agreeable as a *partie-carrée*, even with nice little bodies like——[*pointing to back room*]. I say, Jack, what a good time we used to have together ! We have had a good many of these *parties-carrées*, haven't we ? Nothing like them, no, that there isn't !

JACK

You're right there. A *partie-carrée* certainly doesn't involve that continual effort to please and entertain which is the essence of a *tête-à-tête*. But I think I shall venture to call this the exception which proves your general rule. Can she go with me, then ?

FRANK

I have no objection ; but I don't know what Annie will say. You'd better ask her.

JACK

I hardly think I am the best person to ask. I was going to mention it just now, when she went for me, just because I kissed that dear little sister of hers. Well, if she doesn't want the girl to go by herself, she can come and chaperon her, and I will make love to *her*, so that Lizzie can come home and tell you all about it, and make you jealous.

43

FRANK

You are perfectly welcome, old chap—perfectly.

JACK

I say, Frank. How about Mrs. Courtree? Fascinating woman, isn't she!

FRANK

Superb, my dear fellow, superb! Genius! Wonderful! Venus cut out of a Titian canvas.

JACK

I thought so. You had better mind what you are about, old boy, and not singe your wings.

FRANK

Ha! ha! [*He goes to drawer and takes out photograph.*] What do you say to that? Isn't she beautiful! Heavenly! See that hair—auburn, rich, luscious and seductive auburn!

JACK

You used to have a liking for that, didn't you? Do you remember . . . . what was her name?

FRANK

Sh. [*With sign to back door. He goes to back room.*]

Come in, girls; don't be silly. Jack has apologised to me, and is dreadfully sorry for what he has done, and just imagine how nice he is! He has got a ticket in his pocket for a box at the Gaiety, and wants us to go there with him! [*To* ANNIE.] Go up to him and say that he is back in your good graces; and here's good news for you, Lizzie—he has promised never to kiss you again.

JACK

For the present—for the present, not altogether. It would not be fair of you to rob a man of his only weapon against so dangerous a foe as that sharp-tongued little minx. [LIZZIE *pouts.*

ANNIE

I am very much obliged to you, I am sure, Mr. Durwen. I fear that neither my sister nor myself will be able to go to the theatre to-night. The fact is—I am expecting a friend here and am bound to stay in.

FRANK

Who is coming to you?

ANNIE

Only the lady from upstairs.

FRANK

Well, she can come another time.

ANNIE

But I happen to have asked her for to-night, and I cannot go under any circumstances. I am very much obliged to Mr. Durwen, but I am sorry I cannot go.

FRANK

You are not going to keep Lizzie at home on account of that old cat.

ANNIE

Lizzie can't go alone, and I have no time. I must copy out your MS.—what you wrote this morning.

FRANK

Well, that won't take you long. I did not write ten lines. That won't prevent your going.

ANNIE

Frank, I am not well. I cannot go. I——

FRANK

Not well? Why that's the first I have heard of your malady. What on earth is the matter with you? And here you've been dancing about!

46

ANNIE

I'm sorry to upset your plans, Mr. Durwen—I really cannot go.

JACK

I am more than sorry that you should be too poorly to go; but you'll come, Frank, won't you? and bring *Miss* Lizzie.

LIZZIE

Oh, Annie!

ANNIE

Lizzie, you know very well that you cannot go. You have never been allowed to go to the theatre. You remember how you tried to persuade father to allow me to take you to see *Lucy Frail;* but he would not hear of it. You have been entrusted to me this evening on the understanding that you do just as if you were at home.

LIZZIE

Oh, Annie! But just this once! They need never know at home. Just this once! I do so much want to go to the theatre. You must come with us. Do, dearest.   [*She goes up and coaxes her.*

47

ANNIE

It is not right of you to ask me, Lizzie. You know
how anxious you were to come here to-day, and you
know that you would never be allowed to come again
if you went to the play.

FRANK

Oh, well, nothing will happen to her. Surely Jack
and I can take care of her; can't we, Jack?

JACK

I should think so; but I do hope Mrs. Donovan
will change her mind, and come as well.

ANNIE

How can you persist in this, Frank? Why do
you place me in such a position? It isn't right
for Lizzie to go with me or without me. You
know very well how ridiculous I think the ideas of
father and mother about the theatre, but, as long
as Lizzie is at home, she must do as they tell her
to do.

FRANK

But to-night she is here and you are her mother.

LIZZIE

Yes! You are my mother and you must let me

go. You know how you always wanted to go; and you did go with Frank, although father and mother objected, and now you grudge me this treat. Dearest Annie, let me go.

ANNIE

Lizzie, if you go, you go without my consent. I have no means of preventing you, if Frank insists upon it; but you will make me very unhappy all the evening.

LIZZIE

You must come with us.

ANNIE

No, that I certainly shall not do. Will you faithfully promise me, Frank, to bring Lizzie home early? She is not accustomed to be up late.

FRANK

Of course I will.

LIZZIE

Oh, that will be jolly, dear, dear Sissy !

[*She kisses her.*

ANNIE

[*To* FRANK.] You know this is wrong, and you should help me to resist it.

FRANK

[*Impatiently.*] Nonsense! We'll take care of her splendidly. Why you go on as if she were the first girl who had ever been to a theatre! I should really like to know what prevents your going as well, if we can't be trusted to look after that precious innocent.

ANNIE

[*Aside to* FRANK.] I do not wish to go with your friend—not after his insolence towards Lizzie. That's the long and the short of it.

FRANK

[*Shrugs his shoulders and turns deliberately to* JACK.] You would like to brush up before you start, would you not? Come in here.   [FRANK *and* JACK *go off.*

ANNIE

Lizzie, dear, do you really want to go? I wish you would stay with me. I shall be so lonely.

LIZZIE

Oh, but dearest Annie, there is the lady from upstairs to keep you company, and you have allowed me to go. You know how much I want to go. Why do you grudge me this great treat? You go so often;

it can't be wicked to go. Why Frank himself is something at the theatre, and Frank couldn't do wrong. It's only because father has never been, that he thinks it a sin to go. You aren't poorly, really, Annie, dearest, are you?

ANNIE

No, Lizzie, it's not that, but after Jack's insolence, you should show him that——

LIZZIE

Oh, but Jack is very fond of me. He told me so. He will marry me, I think. Yes, I think he will.

ANNIE

Nonsense, Lizzie; you must put such nonsense out of your head. Father would never let you marry that man.

LIZZIE

Why not? Why should he not? And if he didn't? He never indulges us children in anything. I should just run away, if he refused, and do exactly as you did.

ANNIE

For God's sake, Lizzie, don't say such things. That —that was all different. Promise me faithfully, Lizzie, that you will do nothing so foolish ; promise that you will do nothing without consulting me.

LIZZIE

Of course I shall consult you. You will help me, and then I can have a big, splendid wedding, with bridesmaids and bells and rice and a big wedding-cake, not a poor little wedding like yours. [*Kisses her fondly.*] My dear old sister. Oh, and then Frank need not repay all that money to Jack. Jack shall give it to me, and I shall give it to you, in return for all the money you used to give me when I first came here—secretly, when father and mother forbade me to come. I bought ribbons and feathers, which I could only wear when I came here, because they would have wanted to know where I got them from if they had seen me with them at home.

> [*She has put on her bonnet, and is now quite ready to start.* FRANK *and* JACK *enter.*

FRANK

Ah, I see we are ready! Isn't it too early to go?

JACK

We might walk along quietly ; a walk will do us good.

FRANK

Yes, you are right. A little fresh air will make us

enjoy the fun all the better. It's hot in here—is it not? I suppose I shall not be wanted at the theatre—not now. It's six o'clock. I should have had a wire by now. I may as well risk it. One can't stay in night and day waiting for wires, can one? Good-bye, Annie—you see I'm not going to *that* woman after all—you old silly. [*Kisses her.*] Cheer up.

ANNIE

You won't be late, Frank—on Lizzie's account.

FRANK

No, of course we shall not be late. We'll come back straight from the play, and give the driver six-pence extra to rattle us along quickly.   [*Exit.*

LIZZIE

[*Kissing* ANNIE.] I will tell you all about it dearest, dearest.   [*Exeunt* JACK *and* LIZZIE.

ANNIE

[*Alone, sighs.*] Why could they not stay at home? It's too bad of Frank—but then he only goes to please Lizzie and Jack—yes, Jack. I wish I could open Frank's eyes. But he sees no evil in him—he is blind and deaf to that man's villainy. I'm sure he must be bad. He—and Mrs. Courtree—oh, what shall I do—what shall I do!

[*She is tidying the room when the door is burst open in a hurry, and* FRANK *reappears, holding a telegram in his hand.*]

FRANK

[*Excitedly.*] There—I've got to go after all. Met the boy as we turned the corner. [*Reads.*] " Call without fail 6.30. Important. Evening dress. Courtree." 6.30, and it's ten past six now.

ANNIE

But where are the others? For Heaven's sake, you have not allowed them to go alone—Jack and Lizzie.

FRANK

They would not come back. They are all right. I'm to call for them. Don't you bother. I'm to call for them after the play, and bring Lizzie home. They did not want me, anyhow.

ANNIE

But how could you, Frank! How could you let Lizzie go alone with that man?

FRANK

What was I to do? They insisted on going on,

54

and I had no time to waste in arguing the question. He'll take care of her.

ANNIE

Frank, why have you done this? You know it is wrong. It was wrong of me to allow it; it was wrong of you to urge it. It was wrong of Lizzie; it was wrong of Jack. It was wrong under any circumstances. But this is unheard-of—terrible. Lizzie at the Gaiety in a box alone with Jack Durwen! Oh, Frank! If anything were to happen to her!

FRANK

You are really too ridiculous, too utterly ridiculous. What has come over you of late? What on earth is to happen to them? Didn't you go often enough with me to the play in the old days and since? You look upon poor Jack as if he were a perfect Mephistopheles. Why, dear me, he is just doing it to please the little girl, and he wanted to please you and me as well. He expected us all to go—thought we should enjoy the nonsense at the Gaiety. He is the best-hearted, dearest fellow in the world. [*He has poured out some brandy.*] And here's to his health. [*Drinks it.*]

ANNIE

Frank, you are taking too much of that; you have had too many to-day.

FRANK

Bosh! I never do anything right according to you. I have got to dress now, and that quickly. Are my clothes in there?

ANNIE

You will find them where they usually are. [FRANK *turns back as if to go off.*] Frank, tell me what is this bond between you and Jack?

FRANK

What is this bond? Weren't we at school together? Wasn't he always a kind friend who stood by me—the influential friend who helped me when I most wanted help!

ANNIE

Are you in his debt, Frank? Do you owe him any money?

FRANK

Who has made you think of that?

ANNIE

Frank, do you owe Jack any money? For God's sake tell me!

56

FRANK

Well, and if I do—a trifling sum between friends—I shall pay him back.

ANNIE

I wish you could afford never to see him again! [FRANK *shrugs his shoulders and Exit.* ANNIE *alone and in despair.*] I ought to have gone with them. If anything were to happen to Lizzie—dear, sweet little darling—and mother and father, oh, what should I do! [*She busies herself with the things on the table.*] And there's Frank going to that Mrs. Courtree; how I hate that woman! And how I shall bless the day when that play is produced! I don't even see what all the critics see in her. She doesn't seem to me so great an actress—she certainly is a very handsome woman—very handsome. [*She has moved over to the sideboard, and removes the decanter and glasses, picks up photograph of Mrs. Courtree which is lying on writing-table.*] Here she is [*with a grimace*], Lilian Courtree. Poor Frank—poor Frank—poor me—— Should I take him at his word now, before it is too late—now. No, no! He is good and true. But have I any longer the right to leave things doubtful? And yet I must—yes I must. It would be contemptible, and I should hate myself. I will believe in him at all risk —at all risk.

57   H

FRANK

[*Calling from bedroom.*] Where are my ties?
            [*She jumps up and runs towards the door.*
ANNIE

Where they always are.

FRANK

[*From inside.*] I have got them. What have you got in your hand there?

ANNIE

Oh, nothing.
      [*He comes in with a tie in his hand, but otherwise dressed.*
FRANK

Where did you find that?

ANNIE

It was over there.

FRANK

Don't you be rummaging about in my papers.

ANNIE

I didn't rummage about in your papers. The picture was lying with its face up on the table, I couldn't help seeing it.

58

FRANK

I am not going to be pried upon by you.

ANNIE

Oh, Frank, do be kind to me.

FRANK

Here, tie my tie. [*She attempts to tie his tie, but doesn't succeed. He turns away abruptly and ties it himself.*]—Like to know what's the use of you—more of a hindrance to a man than a help. [*He has tied his tie, and comes up to sideboard.*] Where's the brandy?

ANNIE

I have put that away, Frank.

FRANK

Damn it—how dare you! [*He opens sideboard and takes out brandy, fills glass, and drinks it. Puts on his coat and hat and goes out of door mumbling.*] More of a hindrance than a help, by Jove!

ANNIE

More of a hindrance than a help—and he doesn't even know.

CURTAIN.

THIRD ACT

*Between three and four in the morning. The Room is
dark, except for the faint light of a lamp which
is on the point of going out.* ANNIE *is dozing on
the sofa, which is made up as a bed. She is
dressed in a long gown and covered up with a
rug. One hand hangs down over the back of
the sofa, holding lightly some sheets of a MS., part
of which has dropped on the floor.*

*Absolute stillness, except for rain which beats against the
window-panes; then the rumbling noise of a heavy
cart in the street.* ANNIE *awakes.*

ANNIE

Have I been asleep? [*Turns up the light, which,
however, grows dim again after a few minutes. She
repeats the operation during the scene until it dies out
entirely.*] Ugh! How cold it is. [*Placing MS. on
writing-table.*] It must be late. [*Examining clock on
chimney.*] What! Half-past three? [*Rushing to
bedroom door.*] Frank! Frank! Not home yet.

63

And Lizzie, oh my God! Lizzie, where are you?—
where are you? What has happened to you? Let
me see: you went to the play—you did, didn't you?
With Jack—you promised Frank to return as soon as
it was over. Oh, my God! I see it all. [*Collapses,
sobbing.*] Lizzie—horrible—impossible. [*Opens window, calls.*] Lizzie! Lizzie! Rain—she is waiting for
the rain to leave off. [*Closes window.*] She could
not have waited till now—four hours since the play
was over. Jack Durwen, give my sister back. What
have you done with my sister? [*A cock crows, then
silence—she sits.*] Let me try to think. Oh, I
cannot; it's too horrible. It cannot be! It must
not be! No, no. Perhaps it is not so. Frank may
be with them. Oh yes. Why, of course Frank called
for them at the theatre and they went to Jack's
rooms—all together—the three, and they have
forgotten how late it is. Frank's playing to
them—one of those beautiful melodies—Chopin or
Mendelssohn or Wagner—yes, Wagner—and they
have forgotten all about me, poor me, sitting up
for them, tired, and nervous, and frightened.
[*Forced laugh.*] Hush! Why should they not
enjoy themselves? How could I think of anything else. Why, Jack wanted me and Frank to go
with them, so he could have intended no wrong?
Supposing I had gone—yes, supposing I had gone.
How ridiculous to worry—but—but—but—oh, my
God! If I have done wrong, oh, my God, do not

punish me in this way, I beseech Thee. Have mercy upon me! mercy upon me——

[*She cries, and dozes off sobbing. The lamp has gone out. There is only a ray of light shining through the drawn curtains, which grows in intensity. After a while* FRANK *enters stealthily, in dishevelled evening dress, trousers turned up. Takes off coat and hat, which are wet. Looking round, discovers figure on sofa. From his appearance, looks, and actions, it may be inferred that he has only just recovered from the effects of drinking.*

FRANK

Lizzie, yes of course, little Lizzie. Good job Jack brought her home. I knew he would! As if I could be bothered to go after them—to-night! Oh Lilian, Lilian, what would the whole world be without you, and why should I trouble about these! With your love—and your kisses. Lilian, I adore you. It—it—— [*Lights candle and moves towards back.*

ANNIE

[*Awaking, glares at him.*] Where have you come from? Where is Lizzie?

[FRANK, *going, shrugs his shoulders.*

ANNIE

[*Jumps up madly.*] Where is Lizzie? Frank, do you hear? Where is Lizzie?

65   I

FRANK

[*Returning.*] For goodness' sake, what is the matter?
I have not got your sister. Where should she be—
asleep, of course, in there, hours ago, in a comfortable
bed, while you have chosen to be uncomfortable on the
sofa.

ANNIE

Frank, I tell you Lizzie has not returned from the
theatre, where she went at your wish with Jack.

FRANK

At my wish! What had I got to do with it?
She is not my sister. I can't keep running after your
sister. That telegram—Mrs. Courtree—business. I
could not call for her.

ANNIE

Frank, do you know what you are saying. You
promised to bring her home—to call for her at the
theatre.

FRANK

But I could not, and that's the end of it. I'm not
your sister's nursemaid. Why did you not go to the
theatre with her? You were asked to go, and you
should have gone. It was your duty to go and
chaperon her, not mine to kick my heels at the door

waiting for them. Besides, I had business to attend to—business, do you hear—business !

ANNIE

You promised me, on your word of honour, to bring her home, and you lied. You deceived me, to let them go together. Oh, I see it all, you coward. You have sold her to that friend of yours—you—you——
[*She faints. Pause.*

FRANK

What are you playing at now ? Come to bed, it's late enough. Annie, what is it ?—fainted. I'm damned !
[*Shakes her, pats her hand, and uses every effort to bring her to ; at last he drops her hand violently, and goes off into bedroom with the lighted candle. After a few moments, he reappears at door in shirt-sleeves. She has regained consciousness and is sitting up, staring wildly round with hand to forehead.*

FRANK

Thought so ! You will oblige me by not repeating that performance ; it upsets me, and it does you no good ; or if you do, I shall pack up my bag and go straight away. I warn you.

ANNIE

Straight away, I know. Straight to her whose

embraces you have barely left, whose kisses are still on your lips, and whose touch and whose scent still cling to you. To her you will go—I know it well enough; but not yet, my friend—not till you have given me back my sister!

FRANK

I tell you, I don't know where your sister is. She'll come back all right. It's raining. She is just waiting till it's over. Ugh! how wet I got trudging home —too late for cabs.

ANNIE

Yes, too late for cabs; but not for my sister. Frank, Frank, what are you doing—what are you saying? I beg, I beseech of you, here, on my knees, Frank, go, find her.

FRANK

How can I find her? I don't know where she is. I tell you that it is the rain that has kept her. She is standing under some porch for shelter.

ANNIE

It is four o'clock now, and the play was over at half-past eleven. She was with Jack. Where is she now?

FRANK

Four o'clock, is it? Suppose she has gone to Jack's
rooms to wait till the rain is over.

ANNIE

Man, do you realise what you are saying? Lizzie,
a young girl, my sister, an innocent girl of seventeen,
in a man's rooms from midnight till four in the
morning. What does that mean, Frank?

FRANK

Probably they could get no cab. I had to walk
home, and got deuced wet. My boots are soaking.
                    [*Goes to sideboard and drinks.*

ANNIE

[*Rising to her full height.*] Give my sister back,
man, or I will not answer for my actions.
                    [*Cock crows second time.*

FRANK

That's right. Shout and wake up the house! You
care a lot about what others say or think of us, kick-
ing up a beastly row like this at four in the morning
in a respectable house.

ANNIE

Give me my sister, man—my sister!

69

FRANK

I have not got your sister. Jack's all right. He is a friend of mine. He would not do anything that was wrong. Some trifling accident has happened, and he has thought it best to put her up for the night.

ANNIE

Then why has he not come here to tell me so? Oh, no, do not tell me what you know to be false—to be ridiculous. He has done no wrong. Your men of the world never do! It's only we women who sin—we who believe you when you are lying—who give up all and everything to you—our body, our very soul—just to gratify a little momentary infatuation on your part. But, by God! I will not stand by and watch the undoing of my sister.

FRANK

Ugh! You are remarkably eloquent in denouncing your sister without a vestige of evidence against her. Besides, what's good enough for you is good enough for her! How do you know that Jack won't be the same to Lizzie that I have been to you?

ANNIE

How dare you say that—how dare you! She could not love as I have loved, poor little thing—a child—a mere child. You coward! You have sold her to him for his gold—you have bartered her away as if she had been your chattel!

> [*She is beside herself, and has seized the glass which he has just filled and is about to drink from. She dashes it on the floor; he pushes her. She slaps his face, and he then catches hold of her as if to strangle her, shakes her, and throws her backwards on to the sofa, from which she rolls heavily on to the floor.*

FRANK

> [*Excitedly turns to writing-table, where he rummages wildly among papers, strewing his MS. about on floor. He takes up photo of Mrs. Courtree and props it against decanter, saluting it as he drinks. Cock crows third time. He then takes glass and decanter, turning to bedroom. Oblivious of* ANNIE, *he stumbles over her form as he totters off. He casts a dull backward glance at her, mumbling.*] Hindrance again—everlasting hindrance!

CURTAIN.

Printed by BALLANTYNE, HANSON & CO.
London and Edinburgh.

List of Books

IN

Belles Lettres

All the Books in this Catalogue
are Published at Net Prices

1894

Telegraphic Address
Bodleian, London

List of Books

IN

BELLES LETTRES

(Including some Transfers)

Published by John Lane

𝕿𝖍𝖊 𝕭𝖔𝖉𝖑𝖊𝖞 𝕳𝖊𝖆𝖉

Vigo Street, London, W.

N.B.—The Authors and Publisher reserve the right of reprinting any book in this list if a new edition is called for, except in cases where a stipulation has been made to the contrary, and of printing a separate edition of any of the books for America irrespective of the numbers to which the English editions are limited. The numbers mentioned do not include copies sent to the public libraries, nor those sent for review.

Most of the books are published simultaneously in England and America, and in many instances the names of the American publishers are appended.

⋘⋙

ADAMS (FRANCIS).
    ESSAYS IN MODERNITY. Cr. 8vo. 5s. *net.*   *[Shortly.*
    Chicago: Stone & Kimball.

ADAMS (FRANCIS).
    A CHILD OF THE AGE. Cr. 8vo. 3s. 6d. *net.*
    (*See* KEYNOTES SERIES.)
    Boston: Roberts Bros.

ALLEN (GRANT).

    THE LOWER SLOPES : A Volume of Verse. With title-page
    and cover design by J. ILLINGWORTH KAY. 600 copies,
    cr. 8vo. 5s. *net.*
    Chicago: Stone & Kimball.

ALLEN (GRANT).

    THE WOMAN WHO DID. Cr. 8vo. 3s. 6d. *net.*
    (*See* KEYNOTES SERIES.)   [*In rapid preparation.*
    Boston : Roberts Bros.

BEARDSLEY (AUBREY).

    THE STORY OF VENUS AND TANNHÄUSER, in which is set
    forth an exact account of the Manner of State held by
    Madam Venus, Goddess and Meretrix, under the famous
    Hörselberg, and containing the adventures of Tannhäuser
    in that place, his repentance, his journeying to Rome, and
    return to the loving mountain. By AUBREY BEARDSLEY.
    With 20 full-page illustrations, numerous ornaments, and
    a cover from the same hand. Sq. 16mo. 10s. 6d. *net.*
                            [*In preparation.*

BEECHING (Rev. H. C.)

    IN A GARDEN : Poems. With a title-page designed by ROGER
    FRY. Cr. 8vo. 5s. *net.*   [*In preparation.*

BENSON (ARTHUR CHRISTOPHER).

    A NEW VOLUME OF POEMS. Fcap. 8vo. 5s. *net.*
                           [*In rapid preparation.*

BROTHERTON (MARY).

    ROSEMARY FOR REMEMBRANCE. With title-page designed
    by WALTER WEST. Fcap. 8vo. 5s. *net.*
                         [*In rapid preparation.*

DALMON (C. W.).

    SONG FAVOURS. With a specially designed title-page. Sq.
    16mo. 4s. 6d. *net.*   [*In preparation.*

D'ARCY (ELLA).

    A VOLUME OF STORIES. Cr. 8vo. 3s. 6d. *net.*
                         [*In preparation.*
    (*See* KEYNOTES SERIES.)
    Boston : Roberts Bros.

DAVIDSON (JOHN).

PLAYS : An Unhistorical Pastoral ; A Romantic Farce ; Bruce, a Chronicle Play ; Smith, a Tragic Farce ; Scaramouch in Naxos, a Pantomime. With a frontispiece and cover design by AUBREY BEARDSLEY. Printed at the Ballantyne Press. 500 copies, sm. 4to. 7s. 6d. net.

Chicago : Stone & Kimball.

DAVIDSON (JOHN).

FLEET ST. ECLOGUES. 2nd edition, fcap. 8vo, buckram. 5s. net.

DAVIDSON (JOHN).

A RANDOM ITINERARY AND A BALLAD. With a frontispiece and title-page by LAURENCE HOUSMAN. 600 copies. Fcap. 8vo, Irish Linen. 5s. net.

Boston : Copeland & Day.

DAVIDSON (JOHN).

THE NORTH WALL. Fcap. 8vo. 2s. 6d. net.

The few remaining copies transferred by the Author to the present Publisher.

DAVIDSON (JOHN).

BALLADS AND SONGS. With title-page designed by WALTER WEST. Second Edition. Fcap. 8vo, buckram. 5s. net.

Boston : Copeland & Day.

DE TABLEY (LORD).

POEMS, DRAMATIC AND LYRICAL. By JOHN LEICESTER WARREN (Lord De Tabley). Illustrations and cover design by C. S. RICKETTS. 2nd edition, cr. 8vo. 7s. 6d. net.

DE TABLEY (LORD).

A NEW VOLUME OF POEMS. Cr. 8vo. 5s. net.
[*In preparation.*

EGERTON (GEORGE).

KEYNOTES. Sixth Edition. Crown 8vo. 3s. 6d. net.
(*See* KEYNOTES SERIES.)
Boston : Roberts Bros.

EGERTON (GEORGE).

DISCORDS. Cr. 8vo. 3*s*. 6*d*. *net*.
(*See* KEYNOTES SERIES).

Boston: Roberts Bros.

EGERTON (GEORGE).

YOUNG OFEG'S DITTIES. A translation from the Swedish of OLA HANSSON. Crown 8vo. 3*s*. 6*d*. *net*.
[In preparation.

FARR (FLORENCE).

THE DANCING FAUN. Cr. 8vo. 3*s*. 6*d*. *net*.
(*See* KEYNOTES SERIES.)

Boston: Roberts Bros.

FLETCHER (J. S.).

THE WONDERFUL WAPENTAKE. By "A SON OF THE SOIL." With 18 full-page illustrations on Japanese vellum, by J. A. SYMINGTON. Cr. 8vo. 5*s*. 6*d*. *net*.

GALE (NORMAN).

ORCHARD SONGS. With title-page and cover design by J. ILLINGWORTH KAY. Fcap. 8vo. Irish Linen. 5*s*. *net*.
Also a special edition limited in number on hand-made paper bound in English vellum. £1 1*s*. *net*.

New York: G. P. Putnam's Sons.

GARNETT (RICHARD).

POEMS. With title-page by J. ILLINGWORTH KAY. 350 copies, cr. 8vo. 5*s*. *net*.

Boston: Copeland & Day.

GOSSE (EDMUND).

THE LETTERS OF THOMAS LOVELL BEDDOES. Now first edited. Pott 8vo. 5*s*. *net*.
Also 25 copies large paper. 12s. 6d. net.

New York: Macmillan & Co.

GRAHAME (KENNETH).

PAGAN PAPERS: A VOLUME OF ESSAYS. With title-page by AUBREY BEARDSLEY. Fcap. 8vo. 5*s*. *net*.

Chicago: Stone & Kimball.

GREENE (G. A.).
> ITALIAN LYRISTS OF TO-DAY. Translations in the original
> metres from about 35 living Italian poets with bibliographi-
> cal and biographical notes, cr. 8vo. 5*s. net.*
> *New York: Macmillan & Co.*

GREENWOOD (FREDERICK).
> IMAGINATION IN DREAMS. Crown 8vo. 5*s. net.*

HAKE (T. GORDON).
> A SELECTION FROM HIS POEMS. Edited by Mrs. MEYNELL.
> With a portrait after D. G. ROSSETTI, and a cover design
> by GLEESON WHITE. Cr. 8vo. 5*s. net.*
> *Chicago: Stone & Kimball.*

HARLAND (HENRY).
> THE BOHEMIAN GIRL, AND OTHER STORIES. Crown 8vo.
> 3*s. 6d. net. (See* KEYNOTES SERIES.) [*In preparation.*
> *Boston: Roberts Bros.*

HAYES (ALFRED).
> THE VALE OF ARDEN, AND OTHER POEMS. With a title-
> page designed by E. H. NEW. Fcap. 8vo. 3*s. 6d. net.*

HEINEMANN (WILLIAM).
> THE FIRST STEP: A Dramatic Moment. Sm. 4to, 3*s. 6d. net.*
> [*In rapid preparation.*

HOPPER (NORA).
> BALLADS IN PROSE. With a title-page and cover by
> WALTER WEST. Sq. 16mo. 5*s. net.*
> *Boston: Roberts Bros.*

IRVING (LAURENCE).
> GODEFROI AND YOLANDE: A Play. With 3 illustrations by
> AUBREY BEARDSLEY. Sm. 4to. 5*s. net.*
> [*In preparation.*

JAMES (W. P.).
> ROMANTIC PROFESSIONS: A volume of Essays. With title-
> page designed by J. ILLINGWORTH KAY. Cr. 8vo. 5*s. net.*
> *New York: Macmillan & Co.*

JOHNSON (LIONEL).
> THE ART OF THOMAS HARDY. Six Essays, with etched
> portrait by WM. STRANG, and Bibliography by JOHN
> LANE. Second edition, cr. 8vo. Buckram. 5*s. 6d. net.*
> Also 150 copies, large paper, with proofs of the portrait.
> £1*s. 1s. net.*
> *New York: Dodd, Mead & Co.*

JOHNSON (PAULINE).
>WHITE WAMPUM: Poems. Cr. 8vo. 5s. *net.*
>*[In preparation.*

JOHNSTONE (C. E.).
>BALLADS OF BOY AND BEAK. Fcap. 8vo. 2s. 6d. *net.*
>*[In preparation.*

KEYNOTES SERIES.
>Each volume with specially designed title-page by AUBREY
>BEARDSLEY. Cr. 8vo, cloth. 3s. 6d. *net.*
>Vol. I. KEYNOTES. By GEORGE EGERTON.
>>*[Sixth edition now ready.*
>Vol. II. THE DANCING FAUN. By FLORENCE FARR.
>Vol. III. POOR FOLK. Translated from the Russian of F.
>DOSTOIEVSKY by LENA MILMAN, with a preface by
>GEORGE MOORE.
>Vol. IV. A CHILD OF THE AGE. By FRANCIS ADAMS.
>Vol. V. THE GREAT GOD PAN AND THE INMOST LIGHT.
>By ARTHUR MACHEN.
>Vol. VI. DISCORDS. By GEORGE EGERTON.

>*The following are in rapid preparation.*

>Vol. VII. PRINCE ZALESKI. By M. P. SHIEL.
>Vol. VIII. THE WOMAN WHO DID. By GRANT ALLEN.
>Vol. IX. WOMEN'S TRAGEDIES. By H. D. LOWRY.
>Vol. X. THE BOHEMIAN GIRL AND OTHER STORIES. By
>HENRY HARLAND.
>Vol. XI. A VOLUME OF STORIES. By H. B. MARRIOTT
>WATSON.
>Vol. XII. A VOLUME OF STORIES. By ELLA D'ARCY.
>*Boston: Roberts Bros.*

LEATHER (R. K.).
>VERSES. 250 copies, fcap. 8vo. 3s. *net.*
>*Transferred by the Author to the present Publisher.*

LE GALLIENNE (RICHARD).
>PROSE FANCIES. With portrait of the Author by WILSON
>STEER. Third edition, cr. 8vo, purple cloth, uniform with
>"The Religion of a Literary Man." 5s. *net.*
>Also a limited large paper edition. 12s. 6d. *net.*
>*New York: G. P. Putnam's Sons.*

LE GALLIENNE (RICHARD).

THE BOOK BILLS OF NARCISSUS. An account rendered by RICHARD LE GALLIENNE. Third edition, with a frontispiece, cr. 8vo, purple cloth, uniform with " The Religion of a Literary Man." 3*s*. 6*d*. *net*. [*In rapid preparation*.

LE GALLIENNE (RICHARD).

ENGLISH POEMS. 3rd edition, cr. 8vo, purple cloth, uniform with " The Religion of a Literary Man." 5*s*. *net*.

Boston: Copeland & Day.

LE GALLIENNE (RICHARD).

GEORGE MEREDITH: some Characteristics; with a Bibliography (much enlarged) by JOHN LANE, portrait, &c. Fourth edition, cr. 8vo, purple cloth, uniform with " The Religion of a Literary Man." 5*s*. 6*d*. *net*.

LE GALLIENNE (RICHARD).

THE RELIGION OF A LITERARY MAN. 5th thousand, cr. 8vo, purple cloth. 3*s*. 6*d*. *net*.

Also a special rubricated edition on hand-made paper, 8vo. 10*s*. 6*d*. *net*.

New York: G. P. Putnam's Sons.

LOWRY (H. D.).

WOMEN'S TRAGEDIES. Cr. 8vo. 3*s*. 6*d*. *net*. (*See* KEYNOTES SERIES.) [*In preparation*.

Boston: Roberts Bros.

LUCAS (WINIFRED).

A VOLUME OF POEMS. Fcap. 8vo. 4*s*. 6*d*. *net*. [*In preparation*.

MACHEN (ARTHUR).

THE GREAT GOD PAN AND THE INMOST LIGHT. Cr. 8vo. 3*s*. 6*d*. *net*. (*See* KEYNOTES SERIES.)

Boston: Roberts Bros.

MARZIALS (THEO.).

THE GALLERY OF PIGEONS AND OTHER POEMS. Post 8vo.
4s. 6d. net.   [*Very few remain.*
Transferred by the Author to the present Publisher.

MEREDITH (GEORGE).

THE FIRST PUBLISHED PORTRAIT OF THIS AUTHOR, engraved
on the wood by W. BISCOMBE GARDNER, after the painting
by G. F. WATTS. Proof copies on Japanese vellum,
signed by painter and engraver. £1 1s. net.

MEYNELL (MRS.), (ALICE C. THOMPSON).

POEMS. 2nd edition, fcap. 8vo.   3s. 6d. net.   A few of the 50
large paper copies (1st edition) remain. 12s. 6d. net.

MEYNELL (MRS.).

THE RHYTHM OF LIFE AND OTHER ESSAYS. 2nd edition,
fcap. 8vo. 3s. 6d. net.   A few of the 50 large paper copies
(1st edition) remain, 12s. 6d. net.

MILLER (JOAQUIN).

THE BUILDING OF THE CITY BEAUTIFUL. Fcap. 8vo.
With a decorated cover.   5s. net.   [*Just published.*
Chicago: Stone & Kimball.

MILMAN (LENA).

POOR FOLK. Translated from the Russian of F. DOSTOIEVSKY.
(*See* KEYNOTES SERIES). Cr. 8vo.   3s. 6d. net.
Boston: Roberts Bros.

MONKHOUSE (ALLAN).

BOOKS AND PLAYS: A VOLUME OF ESSAYS ON MEREDITH,
BORROW, IBSEN AND OTHERS.   400 copies, crown 8vo.
5s. net.
Philadelphia: J. B. Lippincott Co.

NESBIT (E.).

A VOLUME OF POEMS. Cr. 8vo.   5s. net.
[*In preparation.*

NETTLESHIP (J. T.).

ROBERT BROWNING. Essays and Thoughts. Third edition,
with a portrait, cr. 8vo. 5s. 6d. net.
New York: Chas. Scribner's Sons.

NOBLE (JAS. ASHCROFT).

THE SONNET IN ENGLAND, AND OTHER ESSAYS. Title-page
and cover design by AUSTIN YOUNG. 600 copies, cr. 8vo.
5s. net. Also 50 copies, large paper, 12s. 6d. net.

O'SHAUGHNESSY (ARTHUR).

HIS LIFE AND HIS WORK. With selections from his Poems.
By LOUISE CHANDLER MOULTON. Portrait and cover
design, fcap. 8vo. 5s. net.   [Just published.
Chicago: Stone & Kimball.

OXFORD CHARACTERS.

A series of lithographed portraits by WILL ROTHENSTEIN, with
text by F. YORK POWELL and others. To be issued monthly
in term. Each number will contain two portraits. Parts I.
to V. ready. 200 sets only, folio, wrapper, 5s. net per part;
25 special large paper sets containing proof impressions of
the portraits signed by the artist, 10s. 6d. net per part.

PETERS (WM. THEODORE).

POSIES OUT OF RINGS. Sq. 16mo. 3s. 6d. net.
                                       [In preparation.

PLARR (VICTOR).

A VOLUME OF POEMS. Cr. 8vo. 5s. net. [In preparation.

RICKETTS (C. S.) AND C. H. SHANNON.

HERO AND LEANDER. By CHRISTOPHER MARLOWE and
GEORGE CHAPMAN. With borders, initials, and illus-
trations designed and engraved on the wood by C. S.
RICKETTS and C. H. SHANNON. Bound in English
vellum and gold. 200 copies only. 35s. net.
Boston: Copeland & Day.

RHYS (ERNEST).

A LONDON ROSE AND OTHER RHYMES. With title-page
designed by SELWYN IMAGE. 350 copies, cr. 8vo.
5s. net.
New York: Dodd, Mead & Co.

SHIEL (M. P.).

PRINCE ZALESKI. Cr. 8vo. 3s. 6d. net.
(See KEYNOTES SERIES.)   [In preparation.
Boston: Roberts Bros.

STREET (G. S.).
    THE AUTOBIOGRAPHY OF A BOY. Passages selected by his
        friend, G. S. S. With title-page designed by C. W.
        FURSE. Fcap. 8vo. 3s. 6d. *net.*
                            [*Fourth Edition now ready.*
    Philadelphia: J. B. Lippincott Co.

SYMONS (ARTHUR).
    A NEW VOLUME OF POEMS. Cr. 8vo. 5s. *net.*
                            [*In preparation.*

THOMPSON (FRANCIS).
    A VOLUME OF POEMS. With frontispiece, title-page, and
        cover design by LAURENCE HOUSMAN. 4th edition,
        pott 4to. 5s. *net.*
    Boston: Copeland & Day.

TREE (H. BEERBOHM).
    THE IMAGINATIVE FACULTY, a Lecture delivered at the Royal
        Institution. With portrait of Mr. TREE from an unpublished
        drawing by the Marchioness of Granby. Fcap. 8vo, boards.
        2s. 6d. *net.*

TYNAN HINKSON (KATHARINE).
    CUCKOO SONGS. With title-page and cover design by LAUR-
        ENCE HOUSMAN. Fcap. 8vo. 5s. *net.*
    Boston: Copeland & Day.

TYNAN HINKSON (KATHARINE).
    MIRACLE PLAYS.   [*In preparation.*

WATSON (H. B. MARRIOTT).
    A VOLUME OF STORIES. Crown 8vo. 3s. 6d. *net.*
        (*See* KEYNOTES SERIES.)   [*In preparation.*
    Boston: Roberts Bros.

WATSON (WILLIAM).
    ODES, AND OTHER POEMS. Second Edition. Fcap. 8vo.
        4s. 6d. *net.*
    New York: Macmillan & Co.

WATSON (WILLIAM).
    THE ELOPING ANGELS: A CAPRICE. Second edition, sq.
        16mo, buckram. 3s. 6d. *net.*
    New York: Macmillan & Co.

WATSON (WILLIAM).
    EXCURSIONS IN CRITICISM; BEING SOME PROSE RECREATIONS
        OF A RHYMER. 2nd edition, cr. 8vo. 5s. *net.*
    New York: Macmillan & Co.

WATSON (WILLIAM).

THE PRINCE'S QUEST, AND OTHER POEMS. With a biblio-
graphical note added. 2nd edition, fcap. 8vo. 4s. 6d. net.

WATTS (THEODORE).

POEMS. Crown 8vo. 5s. net.   [*In preparation.*
There will also be an Edition de Luxe *of this volume, printed
at the Kelmscott Press.*

WHARTON (H.T.).

SAPPHO. Memoir, text, selected renderings, and a literal translation by HENRY THORNTON WHARTON. With Three
illustrations, fcap. 8vo. 7s. 6d. net.   [*In preparation.*

WILDE (OSCAR).

THE SPHINX. A Poem. Decorated throughout in line and
colour and bound in a design by CHARLES RICKETTS.
250 copies, £2 2s. net.   25 copies large paper, £5 5s. net.
Boston: Copeland & Day.

WILDE (OSCAR).

The incomparable and ingenious history of Mr. W. H., being
the true secret of Shakespear's sonnets, now for the first
time here fully set forth. With initial letters and cover
design by CHARLES RICKETTS. 500 copies, 10s. 6d. net.
Also 50 copies large paper, 21s. net.   [*In preparation.*

WILDE (OSCAR).

DRAMATIC WORKS, now printed for the first time. With a
specially designed binding to each volume, by CHARLES
SHANNON. 500 copies, sm. 4to, 7s. 6d. net per vol.
Also 50 copies large paper, 15s. net per vol.
Vol. I. LADY WINDERMERE'S FAN. A comedy in four acts.
                                          [*Out of print.*
Vol. II. A WOMAN OF NO IMPORTANCE. A comedy in four
acts.   [*Just published.*
Vol. III. THE DUCHESS OF PADUA. A blank verse tragedy in
five acts.   [*Very shortly.*
Boston: Copeland & Day.

WILDE (OSCAR).

SALOME: A TRAGEDY IN ONE ACT, done into English, with
10 illustrations, title-page, tail-piece, and cover design by
AUBREY BEARDSLEY. 500 copies, sm. 4to. 15s. net. Also
100 copies large paper, 30s. net.
Boston: Copeland & Day.

The Yellow Book.

An Illustrated Quarterly.

VOL. I.   Fourth Edition, pott 4to, 272 pages, 15 Illustrations, Decorative Cloth Cover, price 5s. net.

The Letterpress by MAX BEERBOHM, A. C. BENSON, HUBERT CRACKANTHORPE, ELLA D'ARCY, JOHN DAVIDSON, GEORGE EGERTON, RICHARD GARNETT, EDMUND GOSSE, HENRY HARLAND, JOHN OLIVER HOBBES, HENRY JAMES, RICHARD LE GALLIENNE, GEORGE MOORE, GEORGE SAINTSBURY, FRED. M. SIMPSON, ARTHUR SYMONS, WILLIAM WATSON, ARTHUR WAUGH.

The Illustrations by SIR FREDERIC LEIGHTON, P.R.A., AUBREY BEARDSLEY, R. ANNING BELL, CHARLES W. FURSE, LAURENCE HOUSMAN, J. T. NETTLESHIP, JOSEPH PENNELL, WILL ROTHENSTEIN, WALTER SICKERT.

VOL. II.   Third Edition, pott 4to, 364 pages, 23 Illustrations, with a New Decorative Cloth Cover, price 5s. net.

The Literary Contributions by FREDERICK GREENWOOD, ELLA D'ARCY, CHARLES WILLEBY, JOHN DAVIDSON, HENRY HARLAND, DOLLIE RADFORD, CHARLOTTE M. MEW, AUSTIN DOBSON, V., O., C. S., KATHARINE DE MATTOS, PHILIP GILBERT HAMERTON, RONALD CAMPBELL MACFIE, DAUPHIN MEUNIER, KENNETH GRAHAME, NORMAN GALE, NETTA SYRETT, HUBERT CRACKANTHORPE, ALFRED HAYES, MAX BEERBOHM, WILLIAM WATSON, and HENRY JAMES.

The Art Contributions by WALTER CRANE, A. S. HARTRICK, AUBREY BEARDSLEY, ALFRED THORNTON, P. WILSON STEER, JOHN S. SARGENT, A.R.A., SYDNEY ADAMSON, WALTER SICKERT, W. BROWN MacDOUGAL, E. J. SULLIVAN, FRANCIS FORSTER, BERNHARD SICKERT, and AYMER VALLANCE.

A Special Feature of Volume II. is a frank criticism of the Literature and Art of Volume I. by PHILIP GILBERT HAMERTON.

VOL. III. Second Edition, post 4to, 280 pages, 15 Illustrations, with a New Decorative Cloth Cover, price 5s. net.

The Literary Contributions by WILLIAM WATSON, KENNETH GRAHAME, ARTHUR SYMONS, ELLA D'ARCY, JOSÉ MARIA DE HÉRÉDIA, ELLEN M. CLERKE, HENRY HARLAND, THEO MARZIALS, ERNEST DOWSON, THEODORE WRATISLAW, ARTHUR MOORE, OLIVE CUSTANCE, LIONEL JOHNSON, ANNIE MACDONELL, C. S., NORA HOPPER, S. CORNISH WATKINS, HUBERT CRACKANTHORPE, MORTON FULLERTON, LEILA MACDONALD, C. W. DALMON, MAX BEERBOHM, and JOHN DAVIDSON.

The Art Contributions by PHILIP BROUGHTON, GEORGE THOMSON, AUBREY BEARDSLEY, ALBERT FOSCHTER, WALTER SICKERT, P. WILSON STEER, WILLIAM HYDE, and MAX BEERBOHM.

Prospectuses Post Free on Application.

Boston: Copeland & Day.